First published 2013 by Brown Watson
The Old Mill, 76 Fleckney Road
Kibworth Beauchamp
Leicestershire LE8 0HG

ISBN: 978-0-7097-2131-4
© 2013 Brown Watson, England
Printed in Malaysia

Classic *Treasury*

Brown Watson
ENGLAND LE8 0HG

Sleeping Beauty

The king and queen were wild with joy. At last, after many years, they had a baby girl. All the fairies came to offer special gifts but the wicked fairy was not invited.

She stormed in, screaming, "When she is fifteen she will prick her finger and die!" but a good fairy whispered: "No, princess! You will sleep for a hundred years until a prince wakens you with a kiss."

As promised, the princess was kind and beautiful but on her fifteenth birthday, she pricked her finger on a needle and fell deeply asleep.

The sleeping princess was laid on a bed decorated with
flowers. Then, with her magic wand, the good fairy touched
everyone in the palace – humans and animals –
and they all fell asleep, too.

Dense brambles grew all around the palace.
After a hundred years nobody remembered it was there
until a young prince fought his way through the thorns.
Suddenly, the brambles parted to let him through.

He found everyone asleep, from the king and queen on their
thrones to the smallest mouse in the kitchen. Astonished, he
wondered what could have happened here.

At last he discovered the sleeping princess. Amazed by her beauty, he gently kissed her. Instantly, the spell broke: the princess awoke to find her handsome prince smiling at her.

Now all the palace folk sprang awake. Soon everyone was celebrating and dancing for joy. Sleeping Beauty and her handsome prince were married straight away – and no one could have been happier.

Bambi

One spring day, a beautiful fawn was born in a forest glade. All the animals, including Thumper, the rabbit, hurried to congratulate Mother Deer and meet Bambi.

Bambi was soon scampering through the trees with
Thumper and Faline, a beautiful young doe. One stormy
day Bambi realised he was lost but his father, the Great
Prince of the Forest, brought him safely back home again.

Winter arrived; so did the hunters with rifles. Terrified animals fled in all directions, but Bambi's mother was shot. Bambi missed her dearly but he still carried on growing and, by spring, even had some little antlers.

Faline had grown up too. Bambi thought she was the most beautiful doe in the world. Two other young deer tried to win Faline, but Bambi proved the strongest and best suitor!

The Prince of the Forest taught Bambi all the forest
secrets – every plant, scent and sound.

Then, suddenly, there was a loud BANG!
Bambi felt a terrible pain in his back. He had been
shot by a hunter. He fled to his father who looked
after him until his wound healed.

By the time he returned to his beloved forest, Bambi was fully grown. He was so excited to meet Faline and all his friends again. Then, one day, the old Prince left. Now Bambi was chosen as the new Prince of the Forest.

Bambi liked to keep watch from the top of a crag, with
Faline always by his side. He was now so majestic
with antlers that rose up like a branching crown.
The little fawn had grown into a great Prince.

Cinderella

A widower adored his daughter, Cinderella, but when he married a lady with two spoiled girls, everything changed. Sadly, he died – leaving Cinderella lonely and sad. Her cruel stepmother and the horrid girls were so unkind.

Cinderella had to sweep, wash, cook and sew.
One day, every young lady was invited to a palace ball.
Hoping the prince might marry them, the stepsisters set
off in great excitement.

How Cinderella wept. She longed to wear a fine dress and dance and meet the prince. Suddenly her fairy godmother appeared. "Don't cry," she said, touching Cinderella with her magic wand: "You shall go to the ball!"

Now in a beautiful gown, Cinderella gasped as the fairy turned a pumpkin into a coach, a cat into a coachman and two mice into horses. "Off you go," she said, "But remember, at midnight my magic will end."

When Cinderella arrived, everyone was amazed by her beauty. Her stepsisters never dreamed that this fine lady was their soot-covered servant – and the prince was in love; he would dance with no one else.

When the clock struck midnight, Cinderella realised the spell would end and fled away. Rushing to escape before she was in rags again she tripped on the staircase and lost one glass slipper.

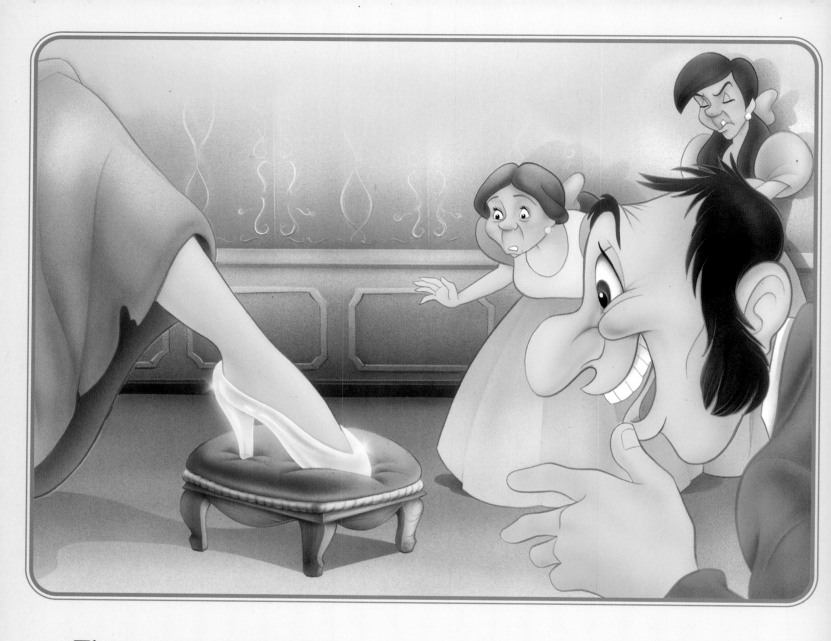

The prince ordered every young lady to try on the glass
slipper. It was so tiny and delicate it fitted no one.
The stepsisters tried forcing it on but it was far too small.
At last it was Cinderella's turn.

"It FITS!" they all cried as she slipped it on. So the handsome prince knew this was his chosen bride. They were married the very next day as everyone celebrated and, of course, lived happily every after.

Peter Pan

All children grow up – all except one, Peter Pan. He lives in Neverland with pirates, mermaids, Fairy Tinker Bell, and the Lost Boys. One night he flew to London and woke up the Darling children – Wendy, John and Michael.

Peter Pan invited them to Neverland: "It's easy to fly; just think happy thoughts." Soon they were gliding beyond the stars to Neverland but jealous Tinker Bell told the Lost Boys to shoot Wendy from the sky.

As their catapults pelted her with missiles, Wendy began to fall
but Peter Pan caught her just in time and told Tinker Bell
never to be so naughty again!

Then he took the children into the cosy Lost Boys' house, where, safe from the pirates, Wendy told them all stories and cared for them like a mother.

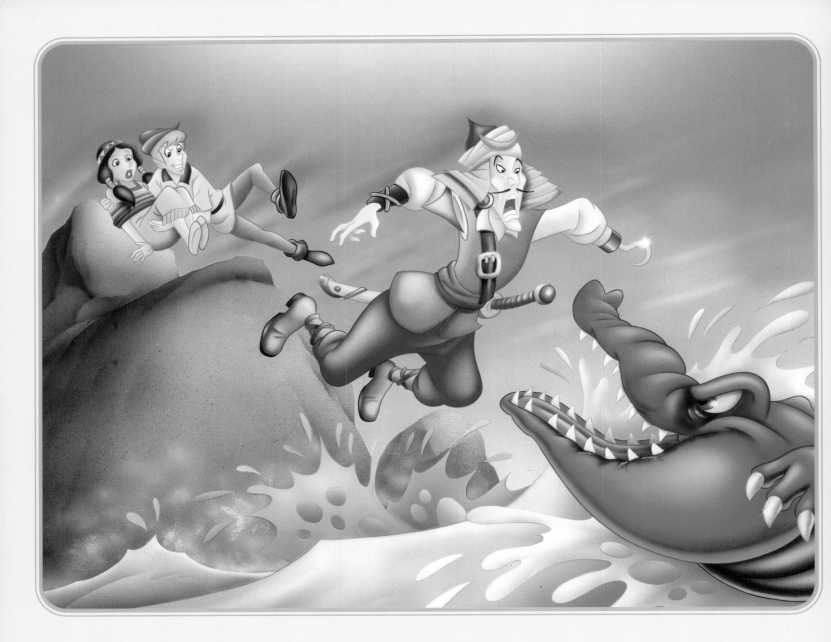

One day, Peter Pan rescued an Indian Princess who had been tied to a rock in the ocean by pirate Captain Hook. Brave Peter Pan saved her from drowning but had to fight Captain Hook and escape the snapping jaws of a crocodile!

Meanwhile, the rascally pirates tried to poison Tinker Bell (but fortunately she recovered) and caught Wendy, John, Michael and the Lost Boys. They marched them off to their ship.

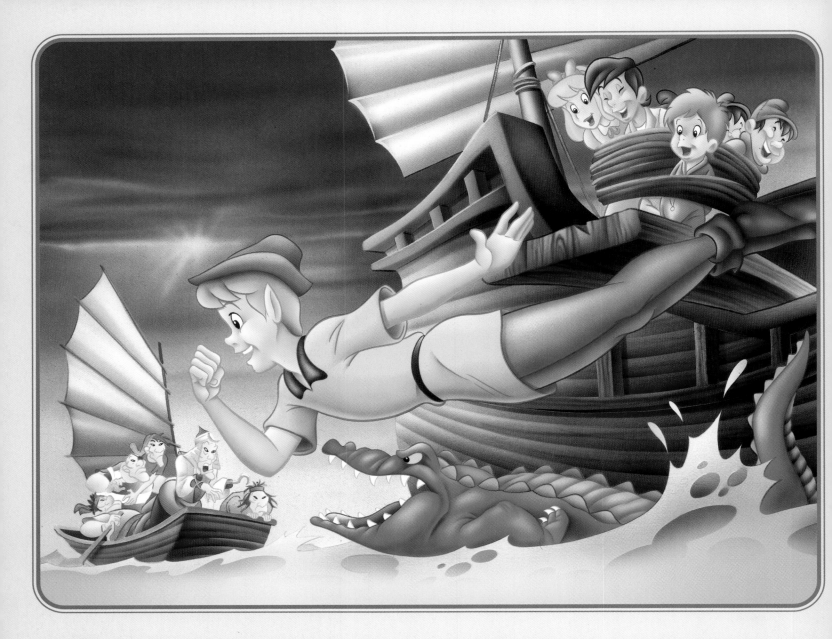

The pirates planned to throw the children into the sea but
Peter Pan came to their rescue just in time. There was a
great battle but, finally, Peter won. Captain Hook and his
pirates rowed away, pursued by the hungry crocodile.

At last it was time to go home. "Stay with us, Peter!" Wendy begged. "No," he said, "I shall fly away now so that I can stay a boy for ever in Neverland but we'll always be friends."

Snow White

Snow White was a sweet young princess in a faraway land. The queen, her vain stepmother, often asked her magic mirror: "Who is the fairest of them all?"
"You are, Your Majesty," the mirror always replied.

Years passed. Then one day the mirror said: "Snow White is the fairest now." The furious queen told her huntsman, "Take her to the forest. Kill her and bring me her heart."

The huntsman liked Snow White, so he let her escape and tricked the queen by giving her the heart of a wild boar instead. Meanwhile, lost and frightened, Snow White ran through the woods until at last she saw a little house.

Snow White opened the door. Inside were seven little chairs and, on the table, seven tiny plates and seven knives and forks. She went upstairs and there found seven little beds. She lay down and was soon fast asleep.

The owners of the house were seven dwarfs who worked in
the mine. When they came home from work that night they
were astonished to find Snow White there. When she told
them her sad story they insisted she must stay with them.

The mirror said, "Snow White now lives
with the dwarfs but is the fairest still." The angry
queen, dressed as an old woman, set off to give her a poisoned
apple. Snow White took one bite and fell senseless to the floor.

When the dwarfs came home, they found Snow White lying
still and as pale as death. They wept as they put her into a
glass coffin – but suddenly a handsome prince came
galloping up. He was amazed to see Snow White.

He lifted her up – and as he did so, the poisoned apple
fell out. Snow White sat up. Oh how happy the dwarfs
were now. The prince married Snow White and everyone
in the kingdom danced for joy.

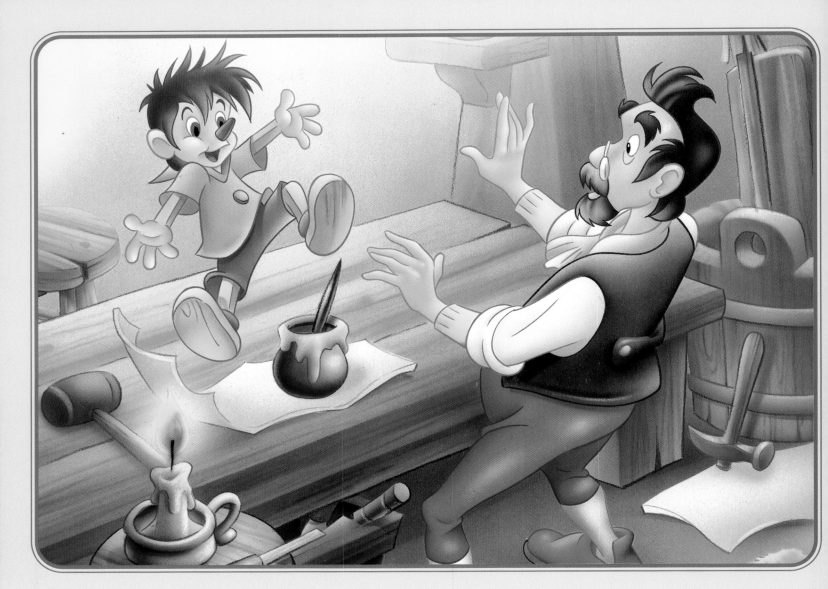

Pinocchio

One day, a poor toymaker called Gepetto made a
fine wooden puppet that he called Pinocchio.
To Gepetto's astonishment, the puppet began to
talk and dance about, just like a real boy!

The next day, Pinocchio, with books and satchel,
set off to school but then stopped to watch a puppet show.
"We must go now," cried his friend, Cricket, but
Pinocchio joined the dancers on the stage.

The theatre owner wanted to keep Pinocchio but the
puppet was suddenly frightened and cried so much
that the man gave him some coins and let him go.
On his way home, Pinocchio met a fox and a cat.

They were thieves. Cricket tried to warn Pinocchio but was ignored again. The rascals said, "Bury your coins in this magic field and you will be very rich!" but once Pinocchio turned his back they stole his money.

Pinocchio was on his way home when a bird told him that Gepetto was searching for him by the sea. Pinocchio did mean to look for Gepetto but then a party of merry children persuaded him to join them and visit Toyland instead.

There he played games and skipped until, suddenly, the fun turned into a nightmare … all the silly youngsters, including Pinocchio, were changed into donkeys.

A kind fairy took pity on Pinocchio and turned him back into a puppet, warning him to behave: "Every time you lie, your nose will grow longer." Pinocchio and Cricket set off to find Gepetto by the sea.

A huge shark swallowed them. Gepetto was inside, too!
When the shark yawned they escaped and swam away.
Pinocchio nearly drowned but was very brave so the fairy
made him a real boy – at last!

Beauty and the Beast

Once upon a time there was a jovial country merchant who lived with his beloved daughter called Beauty.

One day, a falling branch in the forest frightened his horse
and it bolted. By the time the merchant had calmed the horse
down, he realised that he was lost, deep in the forest.

As night fell, the merchant stumbled across a mysterious castle. He knocked at the door. Nobody answered, so he let himself in and fell asleep on the floor. Waking early the next day, the merchant explored the gardens.

He was picking a rose for Beauty when a Beast roared:
"You sleep here and steal my flowers! You must die!"
"Please let me say goodbye to my daughter," the
merchant begged. "Bring her to me," called the Beast.

So the merchant brought Beauty to the castle. She fell to her knees and begged the Beast to spare her father, "Please let him go. I will stay in his place." The girl was very afraid, but the monster treated her kindly.

In fact, the Beast had fallen in love with Beauty and in time asked her to marry him. "I cannot," said Beauty, "But I am happy to be your good friend … and, I beg you, may I visit my father? I promise to return soon."

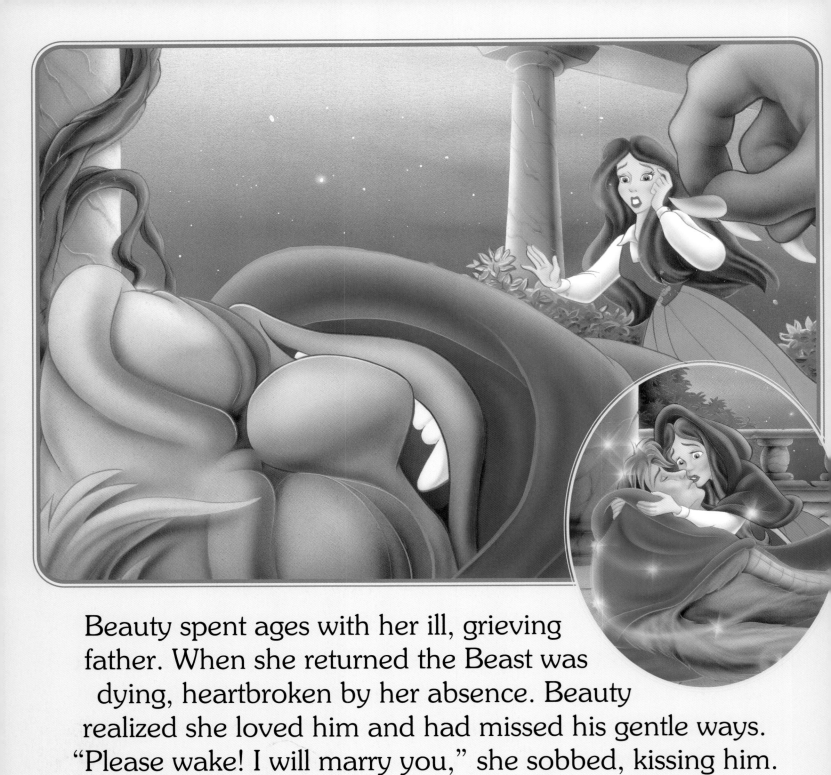

Beauty spent ages with her ill, grieving
father. When she returned the Beast was
dying, heartbroken by her absence. Beauty
realized she loved him and had missed his gentle ways.
"Please wake! I will marry you," she sobbed, kissing him.

Instantly, the monster turned into a handsome prince. An
evil witch's spell had made him a beast – cursed until he
found true love. Now Beauty had followed her heart, not
her eyes – and they lived happily ever after.

The Jungle Book

Once, a wolf found an abandoned baby,
a man-cub, crying in the jungle. He took it home and
the mother wolf brought up Mowgli with her own cubs.

Shere Khan, the terrible tiger, hated people and vowed to kill Mowgli. The boy's friends (Akela, the wolf, Bagheera the clever panther, and Baloo the wise bear) promised to protect him and teach him the jungle secrets.

Mowgli learned the language of the animals and when evil
monkeys captured him, his jungle friends came to his rescue.
Again Shere Khan threatened to kill him but Mowgli sent
charging buffalo to trample the tiger.

Mowgli joined his elephant friend, Hathi, as a new jungle king, respected and feared by all. One day ravenous wild dogs invaded, killing many animals, but Mowgli enticed them into a huge swarm of bees, that stung them ferociously.

Spring arrived. For the first time, as the only human in the jungle, Mowgli felt lonely. He walked until he saw a village with children playing. He heard songs and laughter and felt a great desire to join his kind.

All his friends agreed that it was time Mowgli lived with other humans in the village now. Perhaps he might find his real mother there; he might even meet his mate. The animals waved goodbye and sang a special farewell song.

As he reached the village, Mowgli saw all the children
who would soon be his new companions. He would miss
his animal friends, of course, and would never forget
them. But now a new exciting life was beginning.

The Little Mermaid

When the little mermaid was allowed to rise to the sea surface for the first time, she swam towards the shore, happy and curious. There she saw a handsome prince and instantly fell in love with him.

"You must forget him! You are a mermaid, not a human,"
her father told her angrily when he found out. But the little
mermaid could not stop thinking about the prince and she
hurried to the sea witch to ask her to give her legs.

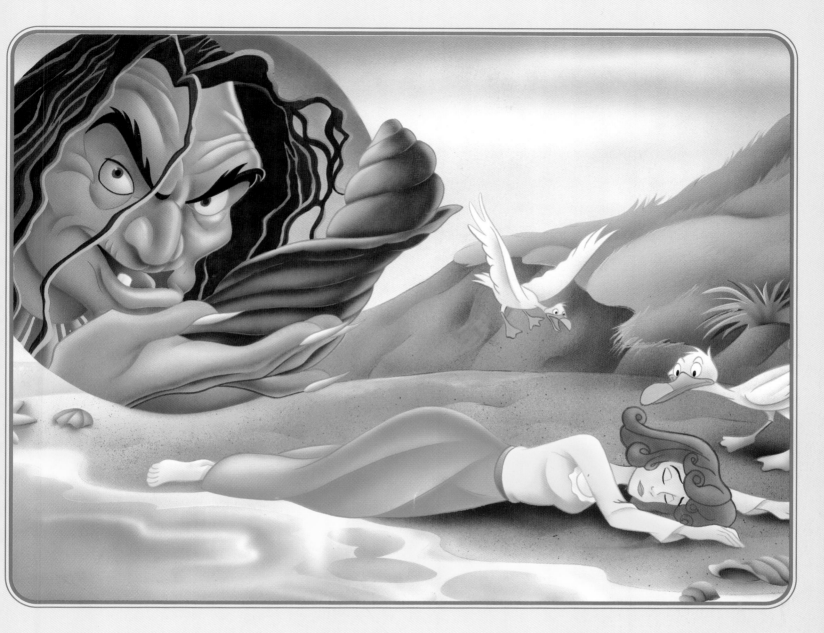

"If that is what you want, so be it," said the witch,
"But every step you take will be agony and you will forfeit
your voice. Also, if you do not marry the prince, you will die."
The little mermaid drank the witch's brew - and fainted.

She woke on a beach to find the prince staring down.
He took her to the palace. They were soon great friends
but, voiceless, she couldn't explain her feelings.
Then the prince announced, "I am to be married."

When she heard this, the little mermaid felt terrible sadness.
One night, while the little mermaid was weeping over her fate
on the seashore, her mermaid friends came to console her.

The mermaids told her that the sea witch could make her a
mermaid again but only by killing the prince with a
dagger. The little mermaid approached the prince's bed with the
dagger… but she could not bear to hurt him.

The day of the wedding arrived, and the ceremony was held
on a boat. The guests were dancing merrily, unaware of the
terrible fate that awaited the little mermaid.

The poor mermaid, mute and alone, threw herself into the water, resigned to becoming sea spray. But when all seemed lost, she did not die, but turned into a sea goddess.

The little mermaid was rewarded for her bravery and
generosity. And ever since then, she has swum through
all the seas of the world, protecting lovers.